Best Bible
STORIES

LOST!

Jennifer Rees Larcombe
Illustrated by Steve Björkman

Marshall Pickering
An Imprint of HarperCollins*Publishers*

Marshall Pickering is an Imprint of
HarperCollins*Religious*
Part of HarperCollins*Publishers*
77–85 Fulham Palace Road
London W6 8JB

First published in 1992 in Great Britain
by Marshall Pickering as part of
Children's Bible Story Book by Jennifer Rees Larcombe
This edition published in 1999 by Marshall Pickering

1 3 5 7 9 10 8 6 4 2

Text Copyright © 1992, 1999 Jennifer Rees Larcombe
Illustrations Copyright © 1999 Steve Björkman

Jennifer Rees Larcombe and Steve Björkman assert the moral right to be
identified as the author and illustrator of this work

A catalogue record for this book is
available from the British Library

ISBN 0 551 03229 4

Printed and bound in Hong Kong

LOST!

For the rest of their lives Mary and Joseph never forgot the **awful** day when they **lost** Jesus. It happened while they were on holiday in Jerusalem. Everyone in Nazareth had locked up their shops and houses, and the whole village had set off together for **the great feast.**

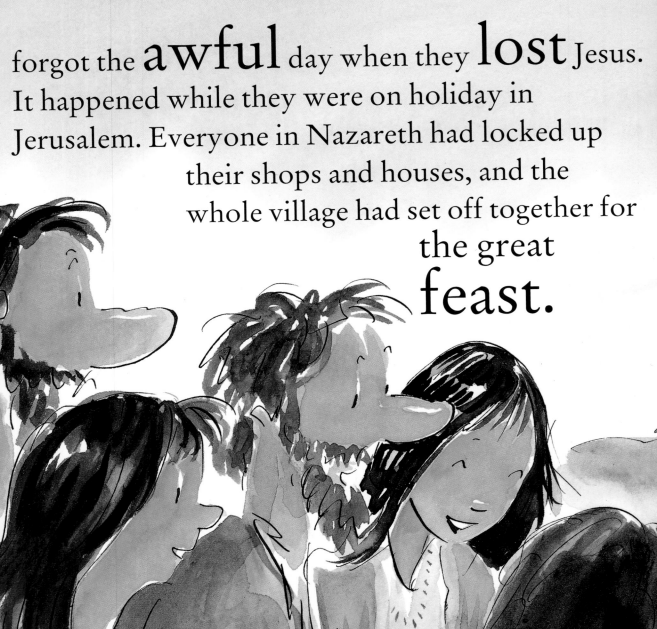

Once a year the Jews all liked to go to the temple so that they could talk to God and give him presents.

Mary and Joseph were so happy as they walked along with their family and friends. In the distance, leading the long procession, they could see Jesus, and clustering round him were all the other children of the village.

'Look at him,' smiled Mary, 'he's so **tall** and **strong** for **twelve.**'

'And always in the middle of a crowd,' laughed Joseph. 'He's **so full of fun**, he makes everyone happy.'

The holiday **flashed** by far too quickly. Suddenly it was the last day and they were all packing up to go home again.

Mary and Joseph were far too busy to notice that Jesus was **missing**. He had gone to say goodbye to the temple and, just for once, he had **gone alone.**

'I feel I really belong here, in my Father's house,' sighed Jesus as he walked round the beautiful building.

'I wish I could stay here for ever, instead of learning to be a carpenter.'

It was just then that he heard the angry voices. A **great argument** was going on in one of the temple courtyards. All the famous teachers in the land were quarrelling with each other about God.

They were far too busy to notice a boy creeping towards them. Yet he actually knew far more about God than they did.

'Who said that?' demanded the most important teacher of all as he spun round and saw Jesus for the first time. The country boy had asked them a question that was so hard none of them could answer it.

'Come here, boy,' snapped the old man. 'If you're so clever, you tell us the answer.'

All day long those teachers fired questions at Jesus, but he answered them all. 'Whoever can he be?' they asked as their white beards wagged in amazement. 'He's not like any other boy in the world.'

By this time Mary and Joseph had set off for home. They thought Jesus must be walking with his friends or his aunts and uncles. It was not until they camped for the night that they realized he was

lost.

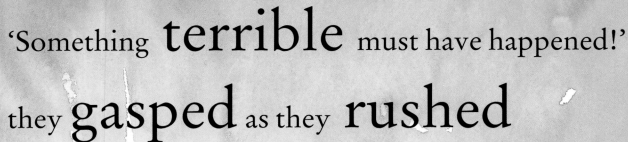

'Something **terrible** must have happened!' they **gasped** as they **rushed back** to Jerusalem.

Of course they should have looked for the

Son of God in the temple,

but they had kept the secret for so long, they had almost forgotten who Jesus really was. Instead they dashed round the dark streets and noisy markets, searching

desperately.

When at last they *did* look in the temple,

they saw a **strange sight.**

A **vast crowd** had gathered round the old teachers, and in the very centre stood Jesus. Everyone was listening to him in amazement.

'You shouldn't have worried about me,' he said gently to Mary. 'Now that I'm twelve I have to work for my

real Father.'

'Come home with us for a little longer,' pleaded Mary.

So Jesus went back to Nazareth and learned to be a fine carpenter.

No one in the village guessed his **secret**,

but everybody loved him.

Luke 2:41-52